One Hell Of A Yule

M.J Knight

This is for all of my fellow smutty freaks that dream of getting railed by Santa and Satan. Hope you have a smut filled Happy Holidays!

Contents

Author Note

This book is written in informal language to make the character's more appropriate for their everyday speech. There will be slang, swearing, and purposely misspelled words to help phonetically set the tone of the storyteller.

If you spot an error or typo that you feel should be corrected, that does not fit the tongue /person's style and manner of speaking, please do not report this to Amazon. I am happy to look into potential corrections if you would care to drop me a quick email at: MJKnightauthor@gmail.com.

Trigger Warning

Let me start by saying there is zero plot in this book. It is pure filthy smut and cuddles. If you are looking for a book to make you think or answer the big questions, this book is not for you!

This book contains strong language, sexual situations including BDSM, and a why choose relationship.

Everything that happens is consensual but this is also a work of fiction.

Please don't try using candy canes as sex

toys or let strangers pierce you body.

Fuck Angels

"**H**e was a complete asshole. Just forget about him. We're here to have a good time!"

I know Tabitha means well, but her voice is getting on my nerves and the drinks are not helping.

"Well, go have a good time then Tabby. I'll be here having another brew and wallowing in self-pity." I snarl, but it goes over her tipsy little head.

"You'll be fine once you find a nice guy to spend some time with. You stay here. I'm going to talk to Seth and see if he has any friends." She says, waggling her brows before spinning on her toes and flouncing off to find her flavor of the week.

I didn't even want to come out tonight. Michael had just sent me the 'let's be friends' text this morning and I wasn't in the mood to be festive, even if Yule had already started.

Yule is normally my favorite time of year, but this year my holly jolly spirit is waning.

"You guarding the drinks?" A deep voice startles me from my self-loathing.

I turn to find a creature that makes my breath catch in my chest.

"N...o.. no! I'm sorry!" I stutter when I realize the giant man is holding a goblet and looking at the cauldron behind me.

His full lips turn up and I can feel my panties dampen at the sight.

"It's okay you're still on my good girl list."

My heart jumps into my throat when my brew-soaked brain puts the puzzle together.

His snow-white hair and beard. The black sparkly eyes. The dark red shirt pulled tight over a wide firm chest.

It's not the Santa mortal children dream about.

I'm weak in knees over Nicolas Klaus.

"Well, I'm glad but I do enjoy being naughty from time to time.

His eyes squint as a deep rich laugh falls from his lush mouth.

Bowl full of jelly, my ass. This man is all hard lines and delicious smelling skin.

"I bet you do. But I'm sure you would be a good girl for me, wouldn't you?"

My insides quiver. Maybe that's where the saying comes from. He turns your insides to jelly.

"I would do my best." I smirk, trying to flirt but my head is still spinning from my overindulgence.

"Crim! Look who I found!" Tabby's high-pitched squeal draws my eyes from the scrumptious giant only to find her pulling over the pathetic elf that we partied with during Samhain.

"I'll see you around sweet girl." Nick's voice teases my ear, but he is gone when I swing my head back around.

Damn it, Tabby!

"Why are you looking at me like that?" Her voice shrinks when I turn my gaze to her.

"I was having a lovely interaction with Nicholas Klaus."

Her eyes pop open in understanding.

"I'm so sorry, Crim! I couldn't see through the sea of people."

"I know. It's not your fault. I was embarrassingly floundering anyway." I sigh.

I wouldn't even know what to do with a man like Nick after spending the last five years with Michael.

He is a literal angel. Wings and halo included. To say the sex had been boring would be an understatement. I mean, I only stayed with him for companionship and to have a plus one to take to parties.

Then, I got that stupid text this morning. He had found another angel, probably Veronica; he always liked to listen to her sing.

So that left me here, at a party with Tabby. All alone, vulnerable and slightly drunk. Thinking that I could bed The Nicholas Klaus.

"No, I'm sure you did great. Go find him and fuck some jolly into your spirit." She tries to encourage me, but now I'm second-guessing everything.

"I don't know. I think I'll just have another drink and just go home."

"Now listen here Crimson North, if you go home, you better go home with Nick. I believe in you and you need this. Don't let Michael be the only one having a good time." She orders, her long finger wagging in my face like I'm a child.

"I don't even know where he went. He said he'd see me around. Was he brushing me off?"

"I doubt he was brushing you off. He knows you could find him easily."

"How could I find him? I don't know his phone number, and I'm not just going to show up at the North Pole and say, 'hey Santa time to dick me down.'" Tabby's giggle is drowned out by the thumping Mariah Carey song. This is a Yule celebration and I still can get away from the damn song.

"No silly. He's basically a demon you can summon him. Duh!"

"Ohhh! That's brilliant! I'll go home and change into my cutest lingerie. Make spiked hot chocolate and cookies. I'll be ready for Santa and I'll get my Yule log tonight!" I don't even have time to laugh with Tabby spinning me around and pushing me towards the door.

"Then go do it, hot stuff! Live your best life and then come back tomorrow and tell me all about it! You better not be walking straight when I see you again." She orders before I'm pushed out the door and into the knee-deep snow.

Now I just have to figure out how to get home!

All I Want for Christmas is Your Dick

C alling a Wuber had been humiliating. A witch that couldn't fly herself home after too many brews. My grandmother would be rolling in her grave.

Falling through the door to my quaint little cabin I'm greeted by the smell of cinnamon and brown sugar.

A mug of cider is nestled in a pile of tinsel on my small kitchen table.

I sway towards it with my arms out for balance and find a note tucked under the ceramic cup.

This one is for good luck! Maybe you can even get creative with the tinsel. ;)

Love, Tabby

She may be pushy and a bit obnoxious, but I do love my elf bestie.

I lift the mug and take a sniff and it smells delicious. Like liquid apple pie.

I drink it down slowly savoring every spice, but notice it leaves a sour note when I'm done.

Instantly my body warms and my nether regions start to tingle. Tabby, you lovely being. The cider isn't spiked with brew. It has Tabby's famous kink potion in it.

Oh well, even if he doesn't come, I'll have a good time by myself.

I rummage through my small closet and dresser until I find my only fancy lingerie. I gather the silky garments and head for the bathroom.

I try to clean off the smells of the party and coat myself in vanilla and brown sugar lotion. It doesn't just smell like fresh cookies. It tastes like them. A little invention of my own making.

I pull on the outfit and check myself in the mirror.

The dark green silk bodice hugs every curve and the flowy black skirt gives it a look of elegance.

My blood red hair hangs in wild curls to my waist as I consider pulling it into a twist but eventually decide against it.

I apply a fresh coat of mascara and lipstick before I approve the look and head to the living room to get my summoning spell ready.

I lay out my candles and draw my sigils. I offer my cookies and bells. The one sure way to summon a demon is offering their favorite things.

I light the candles and think about the delicious man while concentrating on his sigil in the middle of my circle.

"I humbly offer these gifts in your honor, Mighty Red One." I begin my connotation, but my words slur and my vision blurs. I should have waited for the brew to leave my system before drinking Tabby's gift.

"I humbly offer these titties, Santa!" I break out in a fit of giggles.

"Oh, great Santa, come gift this lonely pussy with your log!" I sway and fall to my knees.

"Santa, I've been a very naughty girl. Why don't you come mark me like the bad girl I am." I murmur leaning over and supporting myself on my palms.

A flash of light and the sound of hooves is the last thing I hear before black engulfs my vision.

"You came!"

Here Comes Satan Claws

Damn, my head hurts! What happened?

My eyes feel like they have sand under both lids, making me rub them until they ache.

Blurry visions jump through my head so fast I can't be sure any of them are real.

Casting a circle and trying to summon Nick, but I didn't finish the spell.

That doesn't explain why I'm not on the floor. I specifically remember kneeling on the floor before passing out, but now I feel the cushioned softness that is my couch under my fingertips.

My eyes might as well have weights attached to them. I could always just go back to sleep and worry about everything later.

"The blue velvet couch is a bold choice." A dark masculine voice comments from somewhere above me making my eyes fly open despite their protest.

The creature leaned over the back of my couch could only be described as sinful.

Creamy white skin adorned with deep red markings contrasts lovely with the coal black hair that kisses his brow.

Lips, a beautiful shade of burgundy spread in a wide almost evil grin, showing off short fangs.

But the most intriguing part about him, his eyes. Big black pupils ringed with shimmering gold halos causing the illusion that the gilded irises are moving like liquid.

"Who are you?" I croak out but can't force myself to move.

"You summon me without knowing my name?" He smirks at a joke that apparently went over my head.

"I'm pretty damn sure you're not Nicholas Klaus." I retort, slightly aggravated that a complete stranger, in my house, has the audacity to make fun of me.

"Little Miss, I can guarantee you I am not dear old Saint Nicky. You can call me many things, but Saint isn't one of them. I hate to inform you, but you summoned the Light Bringer, the Father of all Evil, The Great Dragon, Satan." He walks to the front of the couch, a small grin teasing his lips as he bows in the same fashion a prince would.

His gaze finds mine from under the mess of hair before he straightens to his full height.

"Dear child, you summoned Lucifer Morningstar."

He straightens his black satin blazer and dusts off his well-fitting pants.

How did I not notice the horns already? They are tall enough; they rub against my ceiling as he sways to my fireplace and throws another log inside.

"I'm pretty sure I would know if I summoned the Devil."

"Would you really? You seemed a bit inebriated when I arrived. Going on and on about your tits and something about a log." He smirks at me over his shoulder and my whole-body heats in embarrassment at the memory.

"That was meant for Santa not Satan! I'm fine now, you can go back to Hell. Thanks for the help." I jump from the couch, pulling my blanket with me. I suddenly feel very exposed in the lingerie.

"Wait a minute, Little Creature. I happen to know Nick and would be happy to arrange a meeting." He winks.

"Oh really? What would that cost me? I know all about you and your deals. I'm not about to trade my soul for a good fuck." I snark, but he just smiles and sits in the armchair across from me.

A heavy thump against the ground startles me and I look down to see a thick red tail draped around his feet, thumping rhythmically, not unlike a cat ready to play with its prey.

"What about a good fuck that's lasts for days and includes the Devil himself?"

"Are you really trying to seduce me right now?"

"Don't look so shocked! You summoned SANTA so you could sit on his lap. I didn't think it would be too far of a stretch that you might be tempted to include me. I do have the lust venom. He doesn't have that!" He acts appalled, but I still see the mischief dancing in his gorgeous eyes.

"Lust venom, huh? That doesn't sound terrible, but still not going to lose my soul for a few orgasms."

"Okay, no soul! How about we make a different deal. I can come and do whatever I please to you once a week." He offers.

"How about every Sabbath?" I counter.

"Okay! That's a deal. Kiss on it?"

But before I can answer he is leaning over me, pressing me back into my couch with his lips a breath away from mine.

"You're going to want to change our deal before the sun rises."

"I won't back out." I stutter when the tip of his tail traces the arch of my foot.

"Oh, I know. You'll be begging me to stay forever. "

His lips crash into mine, the growl coming from his throat vibrating me to my core.

As quick as he came, he's gone again. Back in the armchair, legs crossed and his tail flipping back and forth in agitation.

"But I must call Nick before the festivities begin."

"You're already here though. Why share me?" I ask, confused and slightly anxious.

"It might be hard to believe, but me and the big man happen to be close friends. He would be awfully mad if he found out I bedded the girl he had been waiting for."

"Waiting? We just met tonight!" He must have the wrong girl. I hope he doesn't back out if Nick does.

"I know you just met him tonight, but he has been

waiting for two Yules now. He was at Michael's party and he hasn't shut up about you since." He rolls his eyes, but I'm still stuck on the fact Santa has been thinking about me.

"Wait, Michael as in my ex-Michael?"

"What other Michael could it be? I will admit that's another reason I was so excited when you summoned me. I've hated that prick for a millennia. Nothing would make me happier than him knowing Nick and I shared you."

I should be pissed, but after Michael leaving me the first day of Yule after years of putting up with his shit, a little petty payback sounds fun.

"Okay give him a call. Let's get the party started." I smirk, feeling a little more confident than I had been.

To my surprise he pulls out a cell phone. He means an actual phone call. I assumed the Devil would have some kind of instant summoning power.

"Hey! I have the absolute best Yule gift for you!" He winks at me and even though it's corny, I blush.

"Yes, yes. I know you are often too busy for your own gifts, but just trust me on this one. You'll love it!"

Before he can even hang up a loud bang rattles my front door.

"What the hell?" I jump, turning towards the commotion.

"More like what in the North Pole." Lucifer snickers at his own horrible joke.

"Who would have thought, Satan can't tell a joke." I muse quietly as he opens the door, revealing the man I've been drooling over.

He has to turn sideways to get his broad shoulders through the door frame.

I hadn't considered an actual giant would ever visit me when I bought my tiny home.

Standing just inside my doorway, snow dripping from his black parka and red beanie, he looks nothing like the St. Nick of my childhood dreams and everything adult me wants to climb like a tree.

"This better be the best present in the world. I have a lot to do this time of year." He grumbles as he brushes off his clothes without looking up.

Lucifer looks back at me with a raised eyebrow, making me realize I'm hiding behind the back of my couch. Nothing but my wild red hair and eyes peeking up from the blue velvet.

"I sure hope she is good enough or you might have just hurt her pride." Lucifer's exaggerated cough has Nick's gaze swinging up to mine.

"Huh... Oh! I'm sorry, I didn't see you there!" His cheeks blush bright red and I'm sure mine matches.

"It's okay, I wasn't exactly making myself known." I chuckle, trying to show off confidence I don't have.

"So, how exactly are you a present for me?" He smirks and my insides melt.

"Technically, this is a shared present." Lucifer interjects. "See, this sweet creature was actually trying to call you to her, but she was a little sloshed and messed up the sigil and then she called to the Mighty Red One. I think you can see where I'm going with this. She wanted Santa but got an anagram of you instead."

If I could crawl under my couch and hide I would. His retelling makes it sound so much worse than I remember.

"Oh. So instead of just bowing out like a good sport, you decided to make a deal and get you something out of the situation." Nick glares towards Lucifer and for a split second his eyes seem to glow.

"I am the Devil. I was thinking a game of Good God, Bad God. Doesn't that sound interesting?" He answers, not a bit deterred by the glowering look.

"I thought both of you are Demons." I say, trying to cut the tension.

"Tomayto. Tomahto. It depends on what religion

you ask. I have been an angel, a god, a demon, a set of beliefs. He..."

"I stay close to the same no matter where you go. Usually, a reason for celebration except for when you're naughty." Nick's gaze is now turned to me and all the anger is gone, replaced with a heat that could incinerate my panties.

"Wait, so does that make you Krampus?" I ask Lucifer.

"No! Mortals like the black and white idea of good and evil. People believe you get jolly Old Saint Nick if you're good and Krampus comes to visit you if you're bad but the truth is..."

"I'm both." Nick says, stepping closer with a smile that shows a fang.

"So, you see, sweet creature, I'm not the only one that comes with built in toys." Lucifer chuckles.

Nick rounds my couch and flops heavily into the armchair, making it squeak in protest.

"Is this what you want? To be extra naughty for Yule?" He asks, leaning forward with his elbows in his knees.

"I mean..."

"Of course, this is what she wants! Who wouldn't want to spend the Holiday spread between two demons ready to pleasure her within an inch of her life?" Lucifer answers for me as he leans in from behind and begins to kiss my neck.

"What he said!" I croak as he nibbles at my collarbone.

"And when the Holiday is over?" Nick's eyebrows raise as he asks the question that makes my stomach sink.

"Then we keep fucking her senseless of course. The choice is hers, Nicholas! You can't assume she's going to fall head over heels for you." Lucifer lectures.

"That's rich coming from the being that told me I would beg for him to stay." I roll my eyes.

"I meant you would beg me to fuck you for the rest of eternity, not that you would want to grow old with me. That's what Nick is referring to. He wants a woman to playhouse with." Lucifer informs me, making Nick's cheeks pink again.

"Not necessarily! I'm just asking if she would consider more than a fuck."

"Yes!" I blurt before my brain can comprehend what I've done. It wouldn't be the worst thing, but I might be jumping the gun.

"Then it's settled! We can discuss this more after everyone's first orgasm!" Lucifer announces before pulling my hair back and working his lips to my ear.

"Focus on how he looks at you. He is completely enthralled, Little Creature." He whispers as he licks the shell of my ear.

And he's right. Nick acts with reverence as he gently takes my foot in his hand and begins working his thumbs into the sole, making me moan.

"I like to take my time getting you worked up while Luce likes to see how fast he can turn you into a soaking wet mess." He comments while rubbing his large fingers from my toes to my heel and up my ankle.

"He's just teasing you. Look at his fingers trailing up your ankle. He wants to bury them in you just as much as you want them there." Lucifer whispers, fingers finding my nipples through my silky top.

"Have you done this before? Together, I mean?" I ask, my breath catching in my throat when Nick's fingers tickle the back of my knee and his lips rub along the top of my foot.

"Once or twice, but we've never wanted the same girl as much as we do now." Lucifer, the ever talkative one, answers.

"I haven't wanted anyone like this in quite some time. That's another reason I'm going slow. I need to savor you." Nick smirks against the skin of my ankle while he draws circles on my thigh.

"He's worried he's going to be a two-pump chump. Good news is, he'll make sure you cum all over that beard a few times before he lets himself go." Lucifer taunts, but Nick just chuckles.

"He's not exaggerating."

"What if I want you to cum fast first and then spend a long time working for your second one?"

"Oh! She is a naughty girl!" Lucifer smiles, letting go of me so he can come sit on the couch.

"No, she's a good girl and will do what she's told." Nick orders, looking up at me from between my knees.

"Or maybe she'll do what she wants. Maybe she'll ride you until you're the one that's a mess." Lucifer catches my mouth with his, working his tongue in and letting me taste the tangy sweetness of him.

"Using your venom isn't very fair." Nick's huffs, leaning back, making me cry out in disappointment but he quickly grabs the other foot to give it equal treatment.

"Venom? That's why you taste like that?" I ask when he eases his tongue from around mine.

"Not quite ripe fruit, I've been told. Yes, that's my venom and it should be starting to work in three… two… one…"

And like a firework going off, sparks begin in my mouth, quickly racing through every nerve from the top of my head to the tips of my toes.

Nick seems to have perfectly timed his licking and sucking of my ankle because the simple act has my panties flooded and my hands reaching for something to steady myself.

"Oh fuck! Fuck!"

"That's a girl. Let us hear how good it all feels. Tell Nick you're going to be our naughty girl tonight." Lucifer growls when I fist his shirt and pull him to me.

"It feels so good. Please don't stop! I'll be a very naughty girl!"

"She doesn't know what will happen." Nick answers, but his voice sounds far away.

"She'll enjoy it!"

"Crimson, you could be a good girl for me. I'll make you feel so good." Nick ignores Lucifer as his nose trails from my knee to the junction of my thighs. His tongue lapping at my panty covered cunt.

"Shhh. Don't listen to him. You want to be bad. Naughty girls get the tail." Lucifer tempts as his warm heavy tail wraps around my free ankle and pulls my legs wide.

"I want to be naughty. I want the tail! I want it all!" I blubber, his venom and Nick's tongue pushing me to my limit.

"I know you do. You're a dirty little slut that wants all the naughty things." Lucifer chuckles, but his words make my insides blaze.

"She likes the name. I can feel her wetness through these silly little things." Nick's fingers toy with the edge of my panties before pulling them to the side.

The cool air feels so good on my heated skin, but it doesn't take long before it's replaced with a hot wet tongue.

"I told you she was bad. Why don't you give her the Krampus treatment?" Lucifer suggests, pushing the green satin from my breasts before lashing my nipples with his tongue, coating them in more of his venom.

"Can she handle it?"

I love how his breath feels against my core. Everything feels amplified and I don't know if it feels like heaven or hell.

Fingers snap in front of my eyes catching my attention.

"Little Creature, eyes on me. I know it's easy to drift into that space, but I want you to feel everything."

I smile, but I'm quickly pulled back to reality when I look between my legs to find Nick with glowing eyes and a devilish smile.

"What's wrong, Red? I thought you wanted to be bad. You know who comes out to play with the naughty girls." He teases.

"Red?" I ask through panting breaths.

"Of course, she would be more curious about the nickname." Lucifer chuckles as he kisses down the side of my breasts and over my ribs.

"The curtains match the carpet. So, you're a true Red." Nick grins, showing off his now elongated fangs.

"I'm Red and you're giving me the Krampus treatment. I think I'm all caught up, now back to what you were doing." I order, letting my head fall back onto the couch.

"Oh no, Red. You're not the boss tonight, but I will give you a few more minutes before we move on." He smiles against my skin, but when his tongue flicks against me it feels different than before.

I cast my gaze back down to him and watch as he tastes me. Before his tongue was wide, flat and warm but now it's thinner, forked and cool to the touch.

He swirls the tips against my swollen clit and I jump

in response.

"Be still, Red. I wouldn't want to cut you before you're ready."

I should be scared of his words, but all they do is excite me more.

"Let me help." Lucifer offers as he grabs my wrists and holds them above my head while his hot tail wraps around my waist, anchoring me to the couch.

I whimper in response but his tongue is back, diving in my mouth and driving me crazy.

"Thank you." The only response from Nick before he's back licking and sucking at the skin between my thighs.

His tongue flicks against my clit again before circling my entrance and diving inside.

"Watch him, Little Creature." Lucifer orders and I obey.

Nick pulls his tongue from me so I can get a good look. It's long, easily ten inches.

"I'm going to taste every inch of you, Red. I want you to let me know how good it feels."

I watch as he tongues the sensitive flesh and the coolness sends shivers up my spine.

"More. I want more." I moan, not knowing exactly what I want.

"I'll give you something, Little Creature."

Lucifer's fingers weave through my mess of curls and gives a steady pull until my head is in his lap.

His other hand works his cock from his pants and it's nothing like I've ever seen.

It's incredibly thick with six rows of shiny silver piercings along the underside and two along the top.

"Open up, Little Creature."

And I'm quick to comply, wrapping my lips around the head and exploring every inch with my tongue.

I moan against his skin when Nick uses two fingers to pump inside of me, his tongue flicking against my clit in rhythm with his hand.

I'm lost in ecstasy when a sharp pinch makes me jerk and my eyes dart back down to the man between my legs.

It might look like Nick, but this creature is lapping at the blood dripping from two small holes on one swollen pussy lip.

His eyes find mine and the animalistic blood covered smile makes my insides twist.

"Your blood is just as sweet as this tight cunt."

I groan around Lucifer's cock as he continues to lick and nibble at my throbbing pussy

"Yes, you are being a good girl, sucking his cock so good. How does it taste?"

It's hard to think. I'm just along for the ride at this point.

"Let me help you."

I open my eyes and Nick is nose to nose with me, mouth open and waiting.

I slide off Lucifer's cock and look up to him, finding nothing but hunger swimming in his molten gaze.

I lean back over and wrap my mouth around the topside of his cock as Nick does the bottom and we meet in the middle. Tongue's wrestling over the cool metal of the jewelry adorning his skin.

"Fuck, yes. You love my venom, don't you?"

When his words sink in, I realize that's the sweet tangy flavor that is driving me mad. I've never minded sucking dick but I would suffocate on him if he didn't pull me back by my hair to catch my breath.

"I think I have somewhere else that needs attention." He moans.

I watch as Nick unlatches from our shared spot on his shaft and slides his tongue down to the slightly red skin of Lucifer's balls. He licks and sucks, making Lucifer's hips buck and his cock sink further into my throat.

A sharp breath from above me

I slide my hand down my body and find my hard nub and begin to rub in circles, building myself up as I watch Nick lick every inch of Lucifer he can find.

"You are being bad. You can't make yourself cum. That belongs to us now." Lucifer says, pulling my hand away even as I cry out for mercy.

"Shhh, you'll get what you want, just keep sucking me down that pretty throat."

He's not joking. Between the venom and Nick working his fingers to make sure he rubs every sensitive spot inside me, Lucifer's cock is sliding down my throat with ease.

He pulls me back by curls when I snarl and run my teeth over the soft skin.

"Are you a feral little witch? Do you need a spanking?"

I can only groan my excitement.

"Nick, I think you have a naughty little whore here that needs some discipline." My pussy clenches on the thick fingers at Lucifer's dirty words.

"Is that so?" He meets my gaze and his eyes are back to glowing orbs, saliva dripping from the fangs that weren't there a minute ago.

"You wanted Krampus." Lucifer's ominous words

ONE HELL OF A YULE

make me shiver.

"You're about to get him, Red." Nick growls as he stands and jerks his shirt over his head displaying deliciously thick muscles decorated with ornate tattoos. I could spend an eternity studying every inch of him but Lucifer is quick to guide my mouth back down on his cock.

"You'll have plenty of time to look when you're riding him later." He growls, lifting his hips to push deeper into throat.

"For now, this is mine." I can't look back to see what he's doing, but I hear the thump of his boots and the clatter of his belt hitting the floor before big hands grab my hips and lift me. He positions me so I can still have my mouth full of Lucifer's cock, but my hips are perched on the arm of my couch, my legs dangling off the side.

"Look at this creamy round ass. I can't wait to turn it red, like the rest of you." He growls.

Lucifer's hand gathers my wrists behind me and his tail secures them to the small of my back, cementing me in place.

It occurs to me that I couldn't get out of this if I wanted to and makes it just that much more toe curling.

The snap of fingers makes me jerk.

"It's okay, Little Creature. That's just Nick using one of his many gifts. Being the master toy maker he is, he can make any kind with just the snap of his fingers." Lucifer explains, using the hand wrapped in my hair to pull me off his cock and turn my head to get a good look at Nick.

Completely nude, his huge cock hard and already dripping, Nick smiles before displaying the long thin riding crop in his fist. Red and white striped like a candy cane, a gingerbread man made of leather sits proudly at the end, just waiting to mark my flesh.

"This should do just fine in that soft rear."

And with that I'm flipped back over and stuffed with hot, venom covered cock again.

I feel big hands spreading my thighs before the leather begins its trail from the base of my neck and down my spine.

"Are you still a bad girl?" He asks, voice deep and full of lust.

All I can do is nod my head as Lucifer thrust his hips making his cock slide further down my throat.

"That's a yes." Lucifer chuckles as I groan around his length.

When the crop trails over my back entrance I moan and try my best to wiggle into the pressure, desperate for release.

"You are a naughty little whore. You want us to feel every hole, don't you?" Nick's words have my pussy dripping. I pop free from Lucifer's cock long enough to beg.

"Yes. Please! I'm a dirty little slut and I need your cock." I plead.

Thwack

Fire crackles where the crop landed and sends tingles straight to my aching cunt.

"You'll take what we give you and your greedy little pussy." Nick growls.

"Yes Sir." I moan.

Thwack

"I didn't tell you to stop sucking that cock."

Lucifer's fist is quick to stuff me full again, hips rocking and filling my throat till I'm choking around the girth.

"That's it, Little Creature. Choke on my cock. You look so beautiful struggling to breathe." Lucifer snarls as he fucks my mouth.

Thwack

I scream around the dick buried in my mouth when the whip lands sharply on my swollen pussy but I push my hips back into the pain and welcome the feeling.

"If I didn't know any better, I would think you were part demon and in heat the way you beg for the pain." Lucifer comments as he holds my head down until I'm struggling for breath. He pulls me back and watches as spit and venom drips from my lips.

"Fuck, you are so beautiful. I want to hurt you, fuck you, make you see hell just to show you heaven." He growls before crushing his lips to mine, sucking my tongue and using his fangs to cut small places in the soft flesh. Copper and fruit fill my mouth but he's quick to lick it up, sucking every drop from my mouth.

Rough hands grasp my hips and turn me again until my knees are on the floor between Lucifer's feet.

"Back to work, Little Creature." He smiles when Nick settles behind me.

"You ready for your present, Red?"

I grunt when Lucifer stands, cock still deep in my mouth. Nick wraps one arm around my waist, the other under a thigh and lifts me to hover over the thick head of his dick.

"We're going to use you like the little whore you are. Hope you're ready, it's about to get rough."

My heart skips a beat at his words but I don't have time to get nervous when he drops me and I'm breached without any warning.

I scream around Lucifer's cock, but he doesn't pull back. He hold my head and fucks my mouth with no remorse.

"Oh fuck! This sweet little cunt is so tight and wet. I feel like I'm going to split you apart." Nick growls behind me as he thrusts up into me.

He's not far off. I do feel like I'm being split straight to my soul. His thick cock works into me over and over while Lucifer pumps into.my throat so deeply tears burn my eyes.

"Look at her. We brought sweet tears to this beautiful face." Lucifer groans.

"She likes being used. She's needed a thorough fucking after being with that angel. How did you stand it? I could see your twisted kinky side a mile away. How did you put up with that missionary only mother fucker?"

He's asking questions he doesn't actually want the answer to. I know what he wants to hear.

Lucifer pulls back long enough for me to feed their ego.

"It was horrible. I've been so horny and both of you are fucking me so good. Thank you. Fuck me harder please. I want your cum. Please. Fuck me harder."

I barely get the last word out before Lucifer is

choking me again, this time with his cock and the hand wrapped around my throat, pushing my head back so he can push every inch of his pierced cock into me.

"Look who's being a good girl now. You'll get your treat when we're finished with you." Nick growls as he pumps into me harder and harder keeping the steady rhythm that's driving me to my own orgasm.

"Fuck, you're clenching so good on my cock."

I feel the swell of his cock deep in my belly, but I can't concentrate on it when something is hitting my mouth trying to stretch my jaw.

My eyes pop open and meet Lucifer's.

"That's my knot, Little Creature. You're going to take that in your ass here soon, but for now you're going to drink all my cum." He grinds between his teeth as he empties himself down my throat.

Nick's hand finds my clit and pinches the same time his cock swells and the combination hits every sensation I need.

I spasm and clench as they continue to pump into me. I feel like I'm floating and falling at the same time. Soaring on the high of my orgasm and feeling the pain of my muscles screaming after being used so thoroughly.

"Fuck Red. You are milking me dry." Nick growls,

grabbing my face and turning it to his when Lucifer slides free.

"I have to taste you like this." His tongue roams my mouth as his hips jerk one last time.

"I'm going to grab us some sustenance while y'all finish up and then we can move to the bedroom." Lucifer chuckles and I can't help but watch his beautiful round ass when he walks away.

"He's gorgeous, isn't he?" Nick remarks while nibbling on my ear.

"He is. It was such a turn on sucking his cock with you." I can't fight the heat that's blazing in my cheeks.

"He's the only man I've ever been interested in. Sometimes I wonder if he had snuck his venom or something in my drink the night we met."

"How long have you known him?" I ask when we finally climb off the floor.

"We met at Cupid's party about fifty years ago. He was trying to pick up women with his tongue tricks. It usually works wonders, but he didn't know Cupid had spiked the punch and all the girls could think about was the winged bastard."

He explains as he wraps an arm around my thighs, lifting me into his big body and as if he has been in my house a thousand times, he takes me to the bathroom.

"The poor guy was distraught. Hell, I was too. Christmas and Valentine's day is my time to shine. So, we spent hours talking and playing brew-pong. We've been pretty good friends ever since."

He lowers my ass to the counter and starts digging through all my bubble bath and body soaps.

"What are you looking for?"

"I know I brought you peppermint body oil last Yule." He grumbles, now bending down to rummage under my sink. I watch as the thick muscles in his back move and flex. I can't stop myself from rubbing my foot over the delicious skin.

"I hate to break it to you, but Michael hates the smell of mint and threw that away the first time I wore it."

"What kind of monster hates peppermint?" He lifts his head from the cabinet looking flabbergasted until he grabs my ankle and places it on his shoulder.

"He said it messed with his sinuses." I murmur as he kisses my calf.

"He's just a whiny little prick. You'll smell lovely on peppermint." He growls into my thigh.

"I think you mean peppermint will smell good on me." I gasp as he bites into my thigh and laps at the blood that leaks from the small wound.

"I always mean what I say. Don't correct me, Red." He stares up at me with those glowing ominous eyes. It's easy to tell when his other side is right on the edge but I don't think he has shown me the real Krampus yet.

"I'm sorry."

"Don't apologize. I just need to hear a yes, Sir." He corrects as he switches to the other thigh to lick and nibble at the soft flesh.

"Yes, Sir." I moan when he bites down again but he's quick to lick and soothe the spot.

"That's my good girl." He smirks, tongue finding my still throbbing sex and licking me until I'm shaking. I have to lean back against the mirror so I don't fall off the sink.

"Looks like I'm missing all the fun."

My eyes pop open to find Lucifer leaned against the door frame with mugs in one arm and a tray full of goodies balanced on the other hand.

"No, just keeping her warmed up for us." Nick answers, but immediately goes back to lick at my folds and over my tingling clit.

"She does look warm. Look at that blush on her tits and throat. You have her burning up."

I am. My whole body is on fire and on edge. I can't

believe how needy I feel right after having a huge orgasm but when Nick pulls back, I'm chasing him, grinding my hips trying to find some friction.

"Come on Red, let's take this to the bedroom."

Nick's thick arm wraps around my waist and before I can think to protest, my world is flipped upside down. I do have a glorious view of his ass while I'm draped over his shoulder.

"Maybe just a nibble." I whisper before rubbing my nose against his flank.

"Don't even think about it, Red. I'm the only one doing the biting between us."

Challenge accepted.

I lick the area lightly before sinking my dull teeth into the thick skin.

"Oh, little girl. You're going to get it now." Lucifer chuckles when Nick jerks.

"You naughty little bitch."

His rough, hard hand connects with my cheeks and I squeal into the skin before biting down harder, drawing a small drop of blood.

"I don't think she cares." Lucifer bends to inspect where I'm latched to Nick's hip.

"She's about to care." I hear the snap of his fingers and my heart drops. Fear and excitement rushing through my already frenzied system.

"Let go, Red."

I just hum around the now copper flavored skin.

"You're in so much trouble, but it's going to be so fucking hot watching you get punished." Lucifer smirks when he uses a clawed finger to pull my mouth from my chew toy.

My arms and legs flail as I'm dropped on my bed but Nick is on me before I can sit up.

"You thought you could be a naughty girl and get the fun treatment you got earlier, but now we're going to experiment with some real punishment."

His face is slightly contorted. Fangs growing at least two inches and poking over his bottom lip. Horns have begun to poke through his snow-white hair and his eyes now glow red as he backs off the bed, letting me sit up.

Lucifer smiles from his side holding ropes of twinkle lights.

"Arm's up, Red." Nick orders.

Should I obey?

I look to Lucifer and as if he can read my thoughts he grins and shakes his head.

I've already made my bed; might as well make snow angels in it.

I cross my arms and lift my chin in defiance.

"Oh, this is going to be fun." Nick growls, grabbing my wrist and hauling me up to a standing position.

He snaps his fingers in front of my face then looks up, making me follow his gaze. A hook that looks oddly like a candy cane protrudes from my ceiling.

"You're going to patch that hole!" I squeal when Lucifer hands him the lights and he begins wrapping them around my wrists in a figure eight pattern.

"I think I'll leave it there. I have a feeling we'll be using it quite often." He smirks when he ties a knot in the lights and feeds the rest through the hook and pulls. My arms are held tight at first but quickly only the tips of my toes graze my bed.

"Doesn't she look so beautiful hanging up for us to do what we please?" Lucifer comments as Nick winds the rest of the lights to my headboard and ties them off leaving me dangling in the middle of my bed.

"She does but this is even better." He snaps again and the lights shine, a rainbow of color casts over my skin, making me into an ornament.

"How is this hot? I can't touch either of you." I protest.

"True, but we can touch you." Lucifer answers but

Nick is looking at me like a puzzle missing a piece.

"I know!" He snaps his fingers and a Christmas ornament pops into his hand from thin air.

"What the hell are you going to do with that?"

"Well, it's about to be used to stop your constant back talk but first I need to ask some questions." He explains but I stopped listening when I realized he was going to gag me.

"Pay attention, Little Creature. This is important." Lucifer orders, the hard flat end of his tail slaps against my thigh and makes me jerk.

"Do you have any hard limits?" Nick asks, rolling the ball gag between his thick fingers.

"I mean, basic ones like don't put a gerbil up my ass. Mr. Lemmiwinks never recovered from that ordeal." I can't help but be a smart ass knowing I won't be able to talk in a few minutes.

"Okay, well what about blades, needles, electrical fun?" Lucifer asks, eyebrows raising, waiting for me to shoot down his ideas.

"As long as you don't knock me out or kill me, I think I can handle it. The potion Tabby gave me earlier is still kicking in my system and pain is quite pleasurable right now." I answer somewhat surprised by myself with how confident I feel considering I've never done anything like this before and I'm hanging naked from my ceiling in front of Santa and Satan.

"My venom will also help if things get a little too intense." He smirks.

"But you will have pain. It is punishment, Red. You fucking bit me!" Nick growls. I can't stifle my giggle when he turns and shows off my bloody teeth marks on his hip.

"That's it. Let's go." He snarls, climbing on the bed and getting nose to nose with me. "If we need to stop jingle this." He whispers as he pushes a small bell into my palm.

"Open up, Red." He smiles, holding up the blue ornament with straps on each side.

I do as I'm told and open my mouth wide so he can push the surprisingly soft ball into my mouth and strap it around my head.

"See you can be nice." He grinds crawling off the bed to stand next to Lucifer.

"Should we leave her here?"

My heart drops and my eyes bulge at the idea of being left hot and needy.

"No, but we can enjoy our snack while watching her squirm." Lucifer chuckles and reaches for the tray of food and the mugs of hot cider.

I watch as they settle on the foot of my bed and snack on cookies and chocolate while talking like I'm not naked in front of them.

"What's your plans for the summer?"

"It is my off time, so I thought about taking a trip to Jamaica or maybe Fiji." Nick answers even as I'm swaying my hips and moaning around the ball, begging for attention.

"That sounds lovely. Would you mind a travel buddy?" Lucifer asks noshing on some delicious looking bruschetta.

"Of course not. I would probably get bored by myself."

"We could keep each other busy." Lucifer winks as he moves the tray to my bedside table before leaning back into Nick and licking the fang still pressed over his bottom lip.

"It would be fun and you would look lovely laid out on the sand." Nick leans into Lucifer's mouth, kissing and licking until the devil purrs like a kitten.

I moan at the sight and fight my constraints. I want to be part of the fun.

"Show me what else that tongue can do." Lucifer begs when Nick finally pulls back showing off the nearly foot long tongue.

"You are naughty by nature." Nick sasses as he grabs Lucifer's legs and pulls until he is on his back across my bed with the larger man fitted snugly between his spread legs.

"Make her see what she's missing." Lucifer smirks in my direction as I try to beg for them to let me down.

I watch as Nick wraps his tongue around Lucifer's cock and begins to pump and squeeze it, making the devil squirm.

"Yes, that feels so good."

Nick's hand comes up to take over the job while his tongue laves Lucifer's balls with his saliva making them tighten. He knows what's about to happen.

I watch as Nick bites the sensitive skin of Lucifer's sack making him jump then quickly moan as Nick sucks the spot.

"Tell me what you want." Nick orders, his forked tongue finding the slit at the top of Lucifer's dick and rimming it.

"That's kind of sensitive." Lucifer admits as his hips jerk.

"Is it?" Nick smirks but doesn't stop. In fact, he pushes until the tip penetrates the slit making Lucifer squirm.

"Yes but keep pumping me and it might be worth it."

Lucifer moans.

Nick does as he's asked. Squeezing and pulling the pierced cock while using his tongue to rim the slit.

Lucifer is a moaning mess. Jerking and thrusting into the huge hand.

"I'm about to cum in your palm." He groans with his head tossed back.

"No, you're not." Nick smirks as he pulls his hand and tongue away, leaving Lucifer pouting.

"That's not very Saint Nick if you."

"I'm only a Saint around children and you're a dirty devil. We have other things to deal with."

Both sets of eyes turn to me and I'm not sure if I want to beg for their touch or run away.

"Did you enjoy our fun?" Nick asks as he crawls towards me in the bed.

I nod in earnest, waiting for my turn.

"Let's see if we can work you up as much as I did Luce."

They each grab an ankle and spread my legs wide, putting my glistening cunt on display.

"Remember how I said you would smell good on peppermint?"

I nod again, anxious to see where this was going.

He snaps his fingers and a candy cane appears in his palm. It's not overly long, but it's very thick with tapered ends and makes me a little worried.

"You do the honors." He passes the huge candy to Lucifer, whose smile grows, reaching his ears.

"Why, thank you!"

He licks the stick end, wetting it, before rubbing it along my dripping slit.

"You did get wet watching Nick play with me. Dirty girl." He smirks, pushing the tip into my pussy, stretching me. It stings at first but when Nick's tongue wraps around my clit, I relax and it slides in with little resistance.

It's only halfway in when the stinging starts to grow. Tingling at first but then uncomfortable. Like that time Michael had used menthol muscle gel and didn't wash his hands before he fingered me.

At least this is on purpose and will end in an orgasm.

"Your pussy is sucking it in, you little slut. Take a breath, the hook is about to slide in that tight ass." Lucifer growls.

I start to panic; I've never had anything in my ass except a pinky finger and even that was a bit uncomfortable.

"Shhh, let me help." Lucifer smiles before ducking

between my legs where I can't see.

I jerk when my cheeks are spread and a wet finger rubs against my tight back entrance.

"Relax, Little Creature. This will make you feel so good."

Nick suctions to my clit the same time Lucifer pushes the lubed digit past the tight ring of muscle and I bite into the ball since screaming isn't an option.

"There we go. You like that don't you?" He purrs from underneath me as he pumps and swirls another finger inside me, followed but the tip of his venom coated tongue.

"Yeah, she does. She's dripping all down the candy cane." Nick smirks, leaning in to lick the sweet confection mixed with my juices.

"Let's try this now."

Lucifer removes his fingers and begins pushing the candy deeper into my pussy until the hook begins to breach my ass and I squirm.

The venom kicks in before the sting has a chance to settle in and to my surprise my body is pushing back to meet the rounded end.

He pumps the candy cane as Nick sucks and nibbles on my clit. If it wasn't for the venom, the blessed potion, and my own sex deprivation I would probably be screaming right now, as the cane bumps against my cervix and stretches my ass wide.

"Maybe she'll be able to take me in her ass without whining now." Lucifer chuckles when I moan and ride the candy hard, begging for more.

"She's so bad. She's about to cum all over us." Nick smiles as I look down and watch his long skillful tongue roll over my clit and slip in beside the candy cane, trailing inside me and rubbing all the spots that make me squeal.

All my muscles burn as the heat builds in my stomach before an explosion rolls through me cramping my toes into points and clamping my pussy down on the candy and Nick's tongue.

"That's it. Cum for us." Lucifer growls as he continues to pump the candy cane inside my trembling body, turning so his mouth is side by side with Nick's. The sight breaks every wall I have left.

All the blood rushes from my head and I feel like I'm being electrocuted and floating at the same time.

Words have no meaning. I'm deaf to the sounds I make. My vision blurs with tears. I scream around the gag in my mouth. My legs thrash, but Nick and Lucifer hold them in place as they lick and suck my cum from my pussy and the drops rolling down the candy cane.

"She needs to taste this." Nick stands and releases

the strap from around my head, slowly pulling the ball from my mouth.

My jaw aches and breathing is a struggle, but he reaches down where the candy and my wet skin meet and gathers the fluid in his fingers.

"Open up, Red. You taste better than any cookie I've ever eaten." He feeds me my cum and he isn't wrong. Sweet, minty and tangy.

"Suck my fingers clean."

I hollow my cheeks and suck all the flavor from his skin.

I moan when Lucifer pulls the rod from my body. I should be beyond satisfied but looking at the pair of delicious naked men in front of me, I realize I'm insatiable.

But also, extremely weak and hungry.

"Time for some after care?" Nick arches a white brow.

"Not quite sure what that means but if it involves food, yes."

"Michael really is a little bitch isn't he." Lucifer says, rolling his eyes as cradles my legs in one arm and back in the other.

Nick detangles the lights letting my stretched and tired arms down to rest against my body.

"We barely had sex and when we did it was pretty boring and uninspiring. He never worried if I finished or not. So, no reason for pampering if I wasn't out of breath and shaking."

"That's the first issue. You should always be out of breath and shaking when you've been with a real man. Second, if he couldn't make you cum with his dick he should have got down on his knees and ate you like you were his last meal." Nick informs me as he grabs the snack tray and mugs from beside my bed.

Lucifer wraps his warm heavy tail around me as he sits, still cradling me in his arms.

"Well. Now I know what I've been missing." I smile when Nick picks up a fat juicy fig and holds it to my mouth.

I bite into it and the sweet juice bursts in my mouth and runs down my chin.

"That was you just a minute ago." Lucifer jokes, wiping up the juice with his finger and sucking it clean.

After everything they have done to me so far, it seems ridiculous but I blush and fight the urge to cover my face.

"She's still all innocent and cute." Nick comments, brushing his thumb over my flaming cheek.

"Michael was my first and we've been together for a while. No big crazy sexcapades going on here." I confess.

"Until tonight and the night is young, Little Creature. " Lucifer purrs in my ear.

"But rest and hydration are important." Nick interrupts, handing me a mug of cider. "No alcohol, but a little something of my own making to help the recovery process and maybe even elevate our next experiment."

I eye the drink, but I've trusted them so far. Why back out now? I gulp the drink down and immediately feel cool and refreshed.

"Why don't you rest your eyes, Little Creature."

"Just for a minute." I yawn curling into his warm chest, his tail hugging me closer.

"When you wake, we'll see just how much you can let go."

Nick's words prick at my subconscious but sleep is already pulling me under into the darkness of my dreams.

Krampus Baby

A cat's tongue wakes me with a jerk. I don't own a cat.

"It's just Nick. Calm down, Little Creature."

I crack one eye open and look down to see someone that resembles Nick. White hair, broad shoulders, strong nose, evil grin.

But where Nick's hair is usually swept back this creature's is a shaggy mess with bright red eyes peeking from behind the curtain of white. His shoulders' red symbols have turned black and grown to take up the majority of his back. Horns have grown to a size that rivals Lucifer's and so has his fangs. They are easily two inches long and could rip through my skin with ease.

I thought his Krampus tongue was strange before, but the real Krampus has a tongue just as long but twice as wide with little prickly spikes covering every inch.

He uses said tongue to lick at my thigh and while it doesn't hurt it is a unique feeling. A cross between sandpaper and one of my succulent cactuses.

"What happened? I was sleeping!" I whisper to Lucifer not wanting any wrath from the angry looking creature between my legs.

"Well, you were moaning and grinding in your sleep and he didn't want to wake you, but it isn't just bad behavior that brings out Krampus. If he ignores his own bad thoughts the alter ego shows up. Somewhat punishing himself. He doesn't mind this side of himself but he would rather be in control, if you couldn't tell."

That was obvious. Nick liked being the one in charge and I'm happy to hand over the reins.

"How do we get Kramp back in the bottle?" I ask, wincing when the prickly tongue goes over the same soft tender skin on my thigh.

"Only one-way, Little Creature. Someone has to get

punished and it sure as shit ain't going to be me."

"What kind of punishment?" I gulp.

"Kramp has some standards. He won't go past your limits." He tries to assure me but it doesn't sound promising. "Are you up for it? If not, I know someone. She has helped in the past."

His words hit me like a punch in the gut. I have zero claim to this demon but the idea of him touching anyone else makes me sick.

"No! I can handle it."

"Then invite him in, sweet girl."

I lean back into his chest and begin to spread my legs, but Nick growls and grabs my thigh with claw tipped fingers, drawing blood where they prick the flesh.

"I'm sorry. I'm just trying to help."

"I don't need your help. I'll do what I please." The voice that erupts from his lips matches his tongue, rough as gravel but still dark and commanding.

He crawls forward over my body, his tongue trailing up my belly and between my breasts as he does.

"You belong to me now." He hisses in my ear.

All I can do is nod, licking my lips as my stomach knots in anxiety and excitement.

"What do you say, little slut?"

"Yes, Sir." I croak out from my dry throat.

He smirks, slinking back down the bed, crouching between my ankles.

"Remember that when I make you scream."

He grabs my ankles and pulls me down in one smooth jerk that makes me yelp.

My head between Lucifer's thick thighs and Nick's head between mine.

"Put your balls in her mouth." He orders Lucifer, but the devil doesn't seem too distraught when he smiles and lifts to his knees.

He straddles my head, knees by my ears and lowers until the soft smooth skin brushes my lips.

"Open."

I feel the strangest compulsion to obey. Not forced, but excited at what might happen next.

My lips part and I poke my tongue out to run along his seam, making him groan and crouch down more.

I begin to suck, lick and nibble the sensitive skin when I feel the prickly tongue back at my thighs. It doesn't stop there though.

Fear and ecstasy duel in my chest when that sharp wet tongue slowly licks up my slit.

Big warm hands grab my knees and pull them up, holding them wide and exposing every inch of me to the lapping.

"How does that feel, Little Creature?" Lucifer asks as Nick circles my back entrance, making me twist away at the painful sensation.

"Let me help a little." I hear him spit, but it doesn't register until the warm venom drips down my pussy and ass, coating me even as Nick does his best to lick it up.

The effect begins but not quick enough. Nick grinds his tongue over my sensitive nub and deep in my cunt, sharp pain and dull pleasure following his movements.

I turn my head and bite into Lucifer's thigh.

"That's okay with me, sweet girl. Unlike Nick, I don't mind the pain. My blood works the same way as my spit and cum. Drink up." He pats my knee sweetly even when I bite down harder and draw blood to lap up.

Soon enough my body is back on fire, heart racing and cunt clenching on the rough tongue as he pumps it into me, licking up every taste of me.

I lick every inch of Lucifer my tongue can reach until clawed fingers wrap around my ankles and I'm jerked to the edge of the bed with Lucifer smiling down at me.

"I'm going to fuck you into tears, Red." Nick snarls, snapping his fingers and conjuring a red and white whip of some sort. Hundreds of little leather straps at one end and a handle in the other.

"What do you say?" He asks, holding the whip up and inspecting the colorful tassels.

"Yes. Sir."

"Good slut."

He brings the whip down on my belly and I scream. Not from pain, but from shock. It stings but not nearly as painful as I expected.

"Do you like that?" Lucifer asks, looking down at me with a raised eyebrow.

I know he would stop everything and put me to bed if I said no.

"Yes." I grin up at him.

The sharp sting hits my breasts.

"Yes what?" Nick growls.

I wasn't aware it applied to both of them but Lucifer's smile grows. He enjoys the submission as well.

"Yes. Sir."

"That's a good girl." Lucifer strokes my face.

The sharp sting hits my thighs several times and I hold back tears of frustration. It hurts, it feels good, it's too much and not enough.

"Look at this sweet little cunt dripping from your flogging." Nick chuckles, running a claw between my folds and gathering my wetness.

"Taste?" He holds it out to Lucifer, who leans forward and licks the finger clean.

"Delicious and ready."

"One more time." Nick sneers, bringing the flogger down on my raw pussy.

I squeal and jerk but can't escape the repeated slaps of the leather on my clit and lips.

"Now you're ready." He throws the whip to the side. "Look at me."

I glance down and for the first time, I see that Krampus has different gear than Santa in many ways.

His cock is now an angry red and has grown in length and girth. The head is wide and the shaft has a swell in the middle. I'm beginning to doubt it will fully fit.

"This is going to hurt so good." He smiles, fangs glinting in my dimly lit room.

He pulls my knees up, wrapping them around his

waist.

"If it gets to be too much, ring the bell." Lucifer orders, pushing the same small bell into my palm again.

"She can handle it."

He fists his huge cock in one hand and spreads me open with the other. He glides the head over my clit and down until it nudges into me.

"Fuck. She is soaked." He groans before pushing in with one fluid thrust of his hips, bottoming out and pushing me up the bed and making me scream. It's all too much. Too big, too hot, too fast.

It's like being split in two with a giant fire poker.

My eyes bulge when he doesn't give me time to acclimate and begins deep, hard thrusts. I didn't think rearranging your guts was real but now I'm questioning that. He pumps into me, hands finding my hips and holding me down into the mattress for leverage.

"Scream for me, Red." He orders but apparently, he fucked insanity into me because I clamp my lips shut and focus on the thump of him inside me.

"She doesn't want to scream so she won't talk at all. Fill that pretty throat up." He orders Lucifer.

"You asked for this, Little Creature" He smirks before assuming the position, straddling my head again but this time he uses a finger to pry my mouth open and feed me his beautiful, pierced cock.

He tilts my chin up, making more room to fuck my throat.

"She needs a necklace to go with these stripes." Nick laughs darkly as he trails his claws over the whelps the fogger left behind.

"She would look beautiful if she were a little blue." Lucifer agrees, wrapping his large hands around my throat and putting enough pressure that his cock feels even bigger in the confined space.

He goes back and forth between squeezing my throat, filling it with his dick then releasing me when he pulls back.

A few seconds of air, a minute of choking. I hate it, but I love it. The burn in my lungs and then the sweet release when I get oxygen. All timed perfectly to the hard thrusting of Nick's hip.

I never thought I would be spit roasted by Santa and Satan, but it's better than I could ever imagine.

"I feel like she's missing something." Nick growls, pinching my nipples between his claws. I would scream if Lucifer wasn't resting his balls on my chin.

"You're right. What could it be?" Lucifer pulls out and I gasp for air.

"Rings?"

"She definitely needs rings!"

"What do you mean rings?" But I'm stuffed full again before anyone answers.

"Right here." Nick says, pinching my nipples again.

"And maybe, here?" Lucifer leans forward to pinch my clit.

"You take top. I'll take bottom." Nick agrees.

I start to twist and for a split second I want to shake the damn bell.

But I don't want this to end. I want to explore and experience it all. I've loved every minute so far and backing out doesn't sound fun.

Mind over matter. Lean into the pain. Whatever that one porn star said that night I got drunk and wandered onto Porndom.

I stop my fighting and try to concentrate on the venom seeping down my throat, the lack of oxygen making me feel floaty and the persistent deep thrusts of Nick's cock stretching my cunt and rubbing the throbbing parts of me.

"You'll be okay, Little Creature. I wouldn't let it hurt." He pauses his thrusts. "Too much."

I hear the telltale snap of fingers as Lucifer releases my throat and reaches for something.

"Breathe through your nose." He orders before dripping venom from his tongue on one nipple, making me jolt in surprise.

He pumps himself in my throat once before pulling out, letting me get a deep breath before sliding in again. He's not quite as deep this time.

He pinches and rolls my nipple between his fingers until I'm grinding down on Nick and moaning around his cock.

He pulls the skintight and I steady myself for the pain to come.

"No biting my dick, Little Creature."

And then it comes. Sharp, stinging, burning pain explodes in my nipple and travels to my stomach making me clench down. That earns a moan from Nick.

"Fuck, that's the hardest anyone has ever squeezed my cock." He growls.

"Next one." Lucifer warns.

And it happens again but I'm better prepared this time, breathing deeply through my nose as my body spasms from the shock.

"My turn."

Lucifer pulls free from my throat and backs up so I can raise my head to see my new piercings.

Two golden rings shine from my sore nipples.

"If I knew you wouldn't ring that bell, I would put three down here." Nick chuckles.

"*Five golden rings.*" Lucifer sings.

"I should ring the bell to escape that horrible joke." I roll my eyes.

"No venom for that little comment." Nick smirks.

"Wait! No! I'm sorry!" I plead but it's too late. Lucifer grabs my wrists and holds them to the bed.

"It'll be over quickly and you're going to love it." He assures me but tears trickle down my cheeks as fear grips my chest.

I could ring the bell. I could stop everything and get cuddles. Then send them on their way but I would regret it. I would always remember the night I gave up. I know my limits and this isn't it.

"Okay." I whisper.

"That's a girl." He smiles, wiping the tears away with his thumb.

"Deep breath." Nick orders and I obey.

I feel his clawed fingers spreading me and pinch my clit up.

"Breathe out."

The moment the air leaves my lungs I feel the needle enter my most sensitive skin.

Pain blooms from my core and swallows me whole.

My brain disconnects from the rest of me and I feel nothing but white noise.

I don't know how long I'm in that space but I'm jerked from it and slammed back into my pain and pleasure-soaked vessel.

"You did amazing, Little Creature."

"I was expecting at least a few screams." Nick pouts.

"I was screaming into the void." I shudder, as the new piercings throb.

"Nick will make you some more of his special brew when we're finished and you'll feel better. You'll still have these though." He says fingers the skin in my neck.

"I left a reminder of how beautiful you looked in my necklace." He winks.

"Sweet talk later. My dick is so hard I'm going to explode if she just as much twitches."

"I want to cum all over this pretty face. Paint you like a gingerbread cookie with my cum." Lucifer growls as he grabs his twitching dick and works it in his fist.

"That does sound fun. I want to do her tits and belly

but first, I need a few more seconds buried in you."

He pushes in deeply, grinding against my throbbing clit, working throaty whimpers and sobs from my lips.

"Show me your tongue, Little Creature."

I look up, past the cock being pumped roughly and into Lucifer's gleaming eyes. I open my mouth, push out my tongue and watch as he pushes his venom mixed spit from his lips.

It gleams as it reflects the festive lights and I see a shimmery green before it lands on my tongue.

"It's concentrated. You're going to be licking my balls in thanks in a few minutes." He smiles as he rubs the head of his cock over my tongue, around my lips and up my nose.

The cock buried in my pussy swells as Nick's thrusts turn slow and hard.

"I'm so close, Red. Cum for me. Squeeze my cock so I can paint you with my essence. Mark you as mine." He grinds out from clenched teeth.

His incredibly long tongue falls from his mouth and winds around my clit the same time the venom starts burning through my veins.

The squeezing of the swollen nub mixed with the perfect grind if his burning cock makes my toes curl.

"She's close to. She's coming undone by the second. Scream for us, Little Creature."

My hands search for an anchor and find Lucifer's hard thighs. I move north, grabbing his sack and massaging.

"Fuck, deeper! I'm almost there."

Nick obliges, grinding into a deep sensitive spot while flicking my clit mercilessly.

"Oh, yes. Just like that. Thank you. Thank you!" I cry out, pleasure constricting my throat.

"You're such a good little whore. Your body was made to take my fat cock." He groans when I begin to cum, clamping down on him.

He stills as I squirm and grind down on him while rubbing and tugging Lucifer.

"Our turn." He growls, kneeling over me and aiming his cock at my chest.

"Finally!" Nick pulls free from my tight cunt and begins jerking off over me.

Searing wet heat splatters my belly, cunt and thighs. His face is a mask of concentration as he works his dick for every last drop.

"Fuck yes." Lucifer says breathlessly, his venom mixed cum splashing my face, neck and chest.

They don't stop, using their cocks to rub every drop where they want it.

"The most beautiful gingerbread cookie." Lucifer smiles down at me while Nick comes to lay down by my head.

"Gorgeous. Marked as ours, just like it should be." He whispers against my lips before sealing them with his.

"Tangy." He sighs, licking some of the cum from the corner of my mouth. "Try mine."

He reaches down and gathers his from my belly and feeds it to me.

I suck his fingers clean, surprised by the taste.

"Burnt marshmallow!"

Lucifer leans down and swirls his tongue over my hip and the patch of red curls above my cunt.

"You could bottle and sell that! Is that how you afford your lavish lifestyle?" Lucifer smirks.

"I don't have a lavish lifestyle, asshole."

"The hell you don't! You have that villa in France and that yacht docked in Tahiti." Lucifer retorts, making my eyes grow wide.

"You have a place in France?"

"It's just a place to visit in the summer. It's not a

big deal." Nick scratches the back of his neck as his cheeks flush pink.

"Sure. A ten bedroom, three story historical home is nothing. Let's not forget the giant conservatory and the garden."

"It's not…"

"I've always wanted to go to Paris." I cut in.

"Why haven't you?" Lucifer asks, grinning.

"Money, time but mostly I didn't know anyone to go with. Tabby doesn't leave town except for funerals and weddings. Michael said France was overrated and boring. He had been there hundreds of times."

"We could fix that." Lucifer's gaze meets Nick's and I can see a lightbulb turn in behind those black eyes. Krampus had some fun and apparently taking a nap for round two.

"We could! Red, go wash off and out in something warm." He orders before jumping up and running to the living room.

"I'll be back shortly. Luce, don't distract her." He yells before my front door slams closed with a bang.

"Come on Little Creature. I'll help you get cleaned up." He smiles, pulling me from the warm bed and pushing me towards the bathroom.

He turns in the water and makes sure it's warm

before helping me step in.

"You wash off. I'm going to find you some clothes."

"Don't be stealing my panties!"

"No promises!"

Hand Necklace Over The Atlantic

The hot as hell fire shower mixed with my homemade body wash worked actual magic on my sore body, but my new jewelry still stings and aches with every move of my body.

I exit the bathroom wearing the yoga pants and hoodie Lucifer left for me. No bra or panties of course.

He is splayed on my couch, large body taking up

three quarters of the comfy blue velvet. Back in his pants and blazer, you would never guess he just spent hours wreaking havoc on my soul.

"Well, don't you look comfy." I tease and he smirks.

"I am feeling pretty darn good after using that sweet little mouth."

"Is Nick back yet?" I ask, looking into my open kitchen but no giant man in sight.

"He messaged. He'll be here shortly. Come sit." He pats his leg.

"I thought this was Nick's job." I joke while falling into his warm body.

"He can have a turn later. Feet." He pats his other leg, so I rest my calves over his muscular thigh and watch as he slips on my tall wool socks followed by my favorite boots.

"Have to keep you healthy and all piggies attached. Demons don't have to worry about frostbite." He wraps his arms around me and pulls me under his chin.

"Lucky I'm a witch though. I have magic for a reason. Survival being the main one." I retort but he just chuckles.

"I get it. You can take care of yourself but isn't it nice to be fussed over a little."

He's right. I haven't had anyone take care of me in years and even though they brought me pain and pleasure that made me think Hell might be better than heaven if all demons are like them, they also took care of me.

"It's been beautiful. The whole experience. I'm glad I got drunk and accidentally called out to the great Satan." I giggle.

"I'm glad you did. It's been a while since I've had this much fun. Watching you come undone between me and Nick has been the best Yule gift I could ask for."

"So, about our deal?" I question, heart racing in my chest. When the night started out, I was just looking for a quick fuck to help get over my self-loathing but now... I don't know what I want but I definitely don't want to stop doing this.

His fingers catch my chin and tilt my face up to his.

"I'll let you be the demon at the crossroads tonight. I'll tell you what I want and you can make the deal. I want this night to last forever." He whispers, molten eyes studying my face.

"Neither do I, but I don't know if I'm ready for anything more. How about we just keep the fun going for as long as we can? No promises, no deals. Whenever it gets boring or bad, we'll just stop and leave it as friends." I counter.

"Okay. I can handle that. I'll just make sure you never get bored or unsatisfied. I'm Satan for Hell's sake! I'm the epitome of a good time."

His lips crash into mine and he floods my mouth with venom that I greedily drink down.

"Just wait and see, Little Creature. I'll make sure you're happy for the rest of eternity."

I start to remind him I'm a witch, powerful but still mortal then I remember he's the King of Hell. He can fuck me senseless even after death and not in the eww kind of way.

"I'll hold you to it!"

The tinkling of bells breaks the comfortable silence we share.

"Looks like the saint is back."

He pats my legs and I climb from his lap to hurry to my door.

Swinging it open, I can't help but gape at the team of reindeer and the ornate wooden sleigh they pull.

"What were you saying about France, Little Creature?" Lucifer whispers behind me, his arms wrapping around my waist and lips meeting my ear.

"This is a joke, right?" I ask watching the huge man climb from the sleigh before checking on the animals.

77

"Nope. This is the real deal, Red." He blesses me with that beautiful smile as he pets the lead deer.

"Enough talking. Time to ride. I've been begging to get one for years." Lucifer says, snatching me up, hauling me over his shoulder and bounding to the sleigh.

"You used me to get a ride?"

"I would use you in all kinds of ways." He grins.

"Fair enough." I shrug my shoulders when he plops me into the cushioned red velvet seat.

He straddles my lap on his way to his seat, the imprint of his pierced cock in my face.

"Already missing your cock, Little One?"

I look up and his gleaming gold eyes and sparkling white smile reminds me, this is what happens when angels learn how to fuck.

With no witty comeback on my tongue, I'm left to nod.

"That's a good girl." He pats my head before taking his seat next to me.

"I made you another." Nick points to a small copper mug sitting on a beautifully carved shelf at the front of the sleigh.

I grab the handle and turn up the cup, drinking

every last drop of the concoction. I now know he holds the secret to being pain free after a pain filled session.

I immediately feel my muscles loosen, my aching nipples and clit ease and I'm able to relax into my seat.

"Thank you." I place the mug back on the shelf and lean into Nick's side when he sits beside me.

"No problem, Red. Wouldn't want you to be too uncomfortable on our trip." He smiles down at me and I can feel the heat in my cheeks.

This morning I was convinced my holidays were ruined and now they are looking to be the best I've ever had.

"How long will it take?" I ask, so excited I can barely be still.

"An hour or so. One of the many perks of being me "

With a flick of his wrist, the reindeer take off, lifting the sleigh high into the night sky.

This isn't my first open air flight; I am a witch after all but I could never go this high in my broom and I'm in awe of the view.

"We're about to go over a city. Look down." Nick instructs as he rests the reins in a hook in front of him.

I lean forward but being small and sitting in the middle doesn't make it easy to get a bird's eye view.

"You can stand. I'm not going to let you fall out, Little Creature."

With the reassurance from Lucifer giving me courage, I stand and look over the edge of the sleigh.

It's breathtaking. Lights shine bright under us just like the stars twinkle above us. A floor made of light for a giant.

"It helps to see the big picture sometimes. Makes our problems seem small in comparison." Nick wraps his arm around my back as he enjoys the view with me.

"I'm enjoying my view." Lucifer chuckles from behind me as he reaches for my hips.

"I know what can make it better."

My pants are jerked down to my knees, exposing me to the cold air.

"Ahhh! It's cold!" I scream, scrambling for my pants.

"I'll warm you up." The warm breath in my cunt lets me know he's already in licking range.

"I'll end up with icicles!"

"Hush, Red." Nick orders, placing one large hand on my back and pushing me over the edge of the sleigh while the other spreads me for Lucifer.

His long scalding hot tongue licks a trail from my extremely sensitive clit to my ass until I'm shaking.

"My turn."

Nick turns me around and lifts me, placing my ass on the edge of the sleigh.

"Have you lost your fucking mind?" I scream as I wobble on the thin ledge, hands grasping at air.

"Have a little faith, Red. I'm not letting you go anywhere except to Nirvana." He smirks as he settles on his knees between my legs.

"You can hold on to me, Little Creature." Lucifer appears at my side with his cock in his hand.

"I'm pretty sure both of you are crazy."

My ranting is cut short when the long winding tongue of the man in front of me wraps around my clit and squeezes the freshly pierced flesh.

"Oh…" I'm caught between a groan and a cry.

"Don't worry about anything but the thrill." Lucifer orders and I try to squirm from the ledge.

The talented tongue laps at every inch of me before working its way into my clenching pussy. Curling and rubbing deep inside me as his fingers push against ass.

"Relax." Lucifer grunts, fisting his cock with one hand and pinching my clit with the other.

"It's hard when everything feels.... so intense." I gasp when a finger breeches the tight muscles and begins working in and out of me in rhythm with the magic tongue.

"It's about to get so much more intense." Nick growls, giving my cunt one last lick before standing up between my legs.

"You're so fucking sweet on my tongue. I could drink you."

I scream when he pushes me back and my world starts to flip but the sound is quickly cut off when both huge hands wrap around my throat and squeeze.

I wrap my hands around his forearms, sinking my nails in and drawing blood.

"I'll let that slide. Fear makes us do things we know we shouldn't." He smirks as he lines his cock up with my entrance and sinks in with one long thrust.

My eyes roll back in my head when he bottoms out and he begins to fuck me like my pussy is the key to happiness.

"Eyes on me, slut." He snarls, squeezing my throat again.

My eyes shoot open when he leans me farther back. The deep thrusting might just push me over the edge. I mean death by sleigh fucking sounds like a good way to go.

Lucifer's gaze meets me over Nick's shoulder. His hand lands on the thick shoulder and pushes him forward and me backwards.

I don't realize what's going on first until I see Lucifer spit and Nick's eyes close.

"Fuck, it's been so long since you let me fuck you." Lucifer groans when he pushes into Nick from behind.

"It's a privilege and this seemed like a good time." Nick's groans.

I feel my pussy clench at the words. It's so fucking hot. Nick thrusts into me the same time Lucifer slams deep into his ass.

I don't know if I've ever been fucked so deeply.

"What do you think, Little Creature? Should I fill his ass up when he cums deep in your pretty little cunt?" Lucifer asks, both hands on Nick's shoulders as he fucks him hard in the ass.

I nod, unable to speak with Nick's hands gripping my throat.

"She loves it. Her pussy is coating me and dripping

down my balls." Nick grunts.

"You like when I fuck Nick? You want me to go harder?"

"I think she's about to cum watching."

Nick's got that right. I feel the beginning of my orgasm building in my stomach.

"Harder it is then." His hands move to Nick's hair as his hips slam into Nick with enough force we are leaned all the way over the front of the sleigh. I bend my head back and see the gleam of water.

We're flying over an ocean.

I have Santa buried so deep in my pussy I'm pretty sure there's a bulge in my stomach while Satan fucks Santa in the ass WHILE hanging out of a sleigh pulled by flying reindeer over an ocean.

This is either a fever dream or the best Yule ever.

The wind whipping my hair, the pull and push of Nick's cock and the squeeze of his hands around my throat all combine pushing me to the edge. The throb of his cock as he empties his seed deep in my cunt and the guttural sounds escaping from Lucifer's clenched teeth throws me over the edge. I spiral down into the depths of orgasm that rips me apart.

The stars above me shine brighter when I open my eyes.

"How's your holiday going so far, Red?"

Nick smiles down at me and my stomach flips.

"It's been okay."

"Oh, just, okay?" He bends over and kisses between my breasts.

"Maybe a little better than okay." I smile.

"We're just getting started, Little Creature."

They pull me up and help pull my pants back on before wrapping me in a soft furry blanket.

"You keep everything in here." I comment, snuggling deeper into the blanket.

"I'm usually alone. I like to get a nap when I can."

"Same. Naps are an important part of any holiday season." I smile when Lucifer wraps an arm around my shoulders and pulls me into his chest

"Then why don't you close your eyes so you'll be rested when we get there."

"Sounds like a plan to me. Wake me when we reach land."

The jingle of the bells hanging from the harnesses lull me into a deep sleep, cuddled up between the two men that changed my life in one night.

Santa Has an Addiction

I dream of sex filled nights and sunny days with two demons that make my heart skip a beat.

"Red, Red. Wake up."

I don't want to open my eyes at first but then the memories flood back. I rub the sleep from my eyes as I sit up to find the Eiffel Tower in view.

We must still be a ways off since it looks two inches tall from where I am.

"Paris!"

"Yep, almost there. Figured we would stop at my place first and put the deer up and then drive into town."

It's only ten minutes before we begin to land.

I gasp as I take in the giant house. Two stories but it looks like it's a mile long with red roof tiles and white brick walls, giving it the perfect French aesthetic.

"It's beautiful."

"Wait till you see the inside." Lucifer grunts as he stands and stretches.

"Why are we all the way back here?" I ask when I notice we are at least a couple hundred yards from the house.

"The stables and the garage are over there." Nick points to the right to a long building that's newer than the house and doesn't fit with the aesthetic at all.

Automatic flood lights shine bright when we glide closer. The deer begin to snort and stomp their feet.

"What can I say? They are a little more spoiled than other pets. The place came with the old barn up there but they need heated stalls with automatic watering and rub bars for after long flights." He laughs and I nod along like I understand.

"Sir! I didn't think we would see you until the spring!" A bright airy voice startles me.

"Sprinkle! Good to see you're still here. Thought you would quit for sure after the last incident with Prancer." Nick smiles at me as he climbs from the sleigh and holds out a hand.

Standing, I find a petite woman with pink hair, bright blue eyes and a fake smile plastered to her cute face.

"He can't run me off that easily Sir." She answers haughtily before strutting to the front of the line and grabbing the bridle of the lead deer.

"I'm glad to hear it. The others have grown quite fond of you. Just don't turn your back on the asshole." Nick laughs as he helps me down and walks me to where the reindeer stand impatiently waiting for the big metal door to slide open.

"I'll bring you out tomorrow to meet all of them. For now, let's get some breakfast and show you around town."

"It's been forever since I've had a real croissant." Lucifer wraps his hand around mine and pulls me to the other end of the building while Nick gives instructions to Sprinkle.

"So, we have to walk to the house?" I ask, eyeing the snow-covered distance.

"It's not that bad. Nick didn't want to add on to the original house. He wants to keep the feel of the place authentic."

"I guess that makes sense. The house has that beautiful rustic look and this place," I look around when we walk through a door into the garage. "Is more modern and high-tech."

Two rows of cars sit inside the building. Lines of lights hang above them, spotlighting each car.

"He likes his modern touches." Lucifer chuckles.

"Seems like it might be an addiction."

"The only thing I struggle with is wanting to be inside you every minute since I've seen you." Nick interrupts from behind us.

"Well, I'm not getting naked until after I've had breakfast."

"Fair enough. I'm starving." He grunts, grabbing my free hand and leading me to a gun metal gray sports car.

"This is my newest toy."

I don't know much of anything about cars but I recognize the Audi symbol. Michael talked about getting one enough.

"It's pretty."

"And fast." Lucifer informs me when he opens the passenger door, climbs in and pulls me into his lap.

"What's the point of having a sports car if it's not fast?"

"What's the point of having fifteen sports cars?" Lucifer's eyebrow quirks.

"He has a point." I turn my gaze to the man that barely fits in the small space.

"I'm a collector."

"You have a problem."

"Let's table my buying habits for the moment and take the poor little witch to eat."

"My stomach is eating itself. I'm growing weak. I think I hear the hallelujah chorus." I pretend to faint, falling back against Lucifer's chest.

"Little Creature, we all know you're not going anywhere near heaven's choir."

"Touché."

"Okay, okay. Breakfast coming right up." Nick laughs pushing the button that cranks the car and peeling out of the garage, tires squealing louder than me.

Catch Me If You Can

"This might be the best thing I've ever tasted." I moan around my bite of chocolate croissant.

Two sets of eyebrows raise at my statement.

"Well, besides Nick's cum. That's not really a food group."

"It can be." His eyebrows wiggle, making me choke on my sip of oat milk latte.

"Don't do that while I'm drinking."

"Don't blame it on him. It's that monstrosity you call coffee." Lucifer balks at my drink like it's hazardous waste.

"I'm sorry I'm not sophisticated enough to drink that jet fuel." I shoot back.

"Ma'am, this is French espresso. Second only to Italian espresso. I can't help it if your palette isn't as refined as mine."

All the while Nick sips his hot chocolate, gaze darting back and forth between Lucifer and me.

"What's next on the agenda?" I ask him, gaining his full attention.

"Well, we can go see the sights?" He offers and I jump at it.

"Yes!"

We spend the day checking out the Eiffel tower, touring the Louvre and standing outside Notre-Dame. Nick promises we'll come back after it's repaired.

I eat my weight in chocolate and bread. Window shop and take pictures to send to Tabby.

The absolutely most perfect day of my life.

"I don't know how I can ever thank both of you." I'm almost in tears when we finally climb back in the car and head back to the house.

"No need for thanks, Red. You deserved a treat after being so good."

"But blowjob's are always appreciated." Lucifer interjects.

"But not required." Nick levels a glare at his best friend.

"Of course not."

I can't help but smile as I lean into his warm chest and watch the snow-covered landscape fly by.

His hands massage and squeeze my thighs, working me up into a squirming mess.

When we finally pull into the garage, I'm back to being a needy little slut but I'm not going to make it easy on them.

Lucifer reaches for me when we climb from the car but I duck his hand and shuffle backwards away from him.

"Feeling playful, Little Creature?"

"Or wanting to be naughty again?" Nick smirks at me over the top of the car.

" I just think I've made it too easy. Both of you should have to work a little for it." I smirk back when Nick's eyes widen.

"Oh really?" Lucifer stalks towards me as I back

towards the open door.

"Yep. You guys are getting complacent. Just telling me what to do and expecting me to do it. Believe it or not, I'm a brat at heart." I peek over my shoulder and make sure my path is clear.

"Oh. We know you're a brat. Just thought we had fixed that already." Nick smiles, fangs growing right along with the cock straining his pants.

"It takes more than a few spankings to tame this brat. I think deep down you enjoy the brat."

"I know I do. I like hurting you, Little Creature." Lucifer growls.

"Good. Then you'll enjoy catching me first." I don't give them a second to think before I sprint out the door and make a mad dash for the house.

The yard between the garage and the house is pitch black but the falling snow looks like sparkles as the flakes reflect the far away lights of the house.

I focus on the lights and run as fast as I can but I can feel their presence. The crunch of snow from both sides of me makes my heart skip a beat. They are close but I can't see them in the dark.

"We're going to get you Little Creature." Lucifer hiss mixes with the wind blowing by my ear and I squeal as I veer to the right.

"I can't wait to use you." The dark voice of Krampus

fighting to be free echo's behind me and pushes me harder.

The back of the house is only fifty yards away but I know they are just playing with me. I'll never make it that far.

"You belong to us."

I hit a brick wall only to have another one plow into me from behind, knocking the breath from my body as I'm knocked to the cold snow-covered ground.

"And we're going to mark you as ours." Nick growls, from behind me before his mouth latch on to my throat and his fangs sink in.

I want to scream but Lucifer already has my mouth covered with his tongue rubbing against mine and drowning me in venom.

Nick's vibrations against my back and Lucifer bugling cock pressed to my stomach makes me squirm in anticipation.

"When we get in, I'll give you my mark." Lucifer grins against my lips.

"Then why wait?" I say between panting breaths as Nick licks the wounds he created.

I'm picked up by thick arms and quickly carried the rest of the way to the house.

As soon as the door closes behind us, I'm dropped,

leaving me to scream until I hit a pile of cushions.

"What the fuck?" I ask looking around.

"I called ahead and had Sprinkle fix us a special place." Nick grins from above me. Eyes that beautiful dark cherry red. His darker side, fighting to get out.

"Well, that was sweet of you." I smile as I lay back into the thick cushions and watch them undress.

"It was supposed to be sweet. We were going to take it slow and make you cum over and over but apparently you want to be used like a dirty little slut."

"I do. We can take it slow later. I've been taking it slow for years. I want it fast and hard. I want everything. Use me and make me scream." I squirm as I work my hand down my body and into my pants.

Lucifer reaches down and jerks my pants from me, leaving me bare and soaking wet for them.

I use my fingers to spread my dripping pussy lips and watch as they fist their cocks.

"Wider." Lucifer growls.

I use my other hand to spread myself further apart for my men. Open with my insides clenching in need.

"Pinch your clit, Red. Make it hurt."

And I do. I pinch the still tender flesh and groan.

"You want me to mark you, Sweet Creature." Lucifer asks as he drops to his knees beside me.

"Yes. Mark me. Claim me." I'm not thinking. I'm lost in the pleasure and the heat of the night.

"Just remember you asked for it." He smirks before his claws grow long in front of my face.

"I'm thinking right here." He runs one sharp point over my breasts. "Or maybe here." He teases the inside of my thigh.

It's the waiting that drives you mad.

He starts to touch me again and I pull my fingers from my pussy to brace myself.

"No. Keep rubbing that sweet cunt if you want me to mark you."

I obey, swirling my fingers over the small ring there and making myself shiver.

"That's it. I don't want you to stop. Even when it hurts."

The tip of his claw drags against my skin so slowly, I can't tell if it hurts or tickles at first. Quickly the sensation turns to a burn.

I try to pull my leg away but Nick has one rough hand wrapped around my ankle, making sure I don't go anywhere.

"Keep rubbing, Little Creature." I didn't realize I had stopped, my brain sole focus being that sharp burning sting at the top of my thigh.

I begin rubbing again and try my best to think about the sweet throb at my clit.

"Done." He leans over and kisses the tender spot before letting me sit up and look at it.

An intricate sigil is carved into the creamy flesh.

"What's it mean?" I ask, dragging my fingers over the wound.

"It's the sigil you used earlier. Mine." He smirks as I turn red remembering the whole drunk call fiasco like it wasn't just forty-eight hours ago.

"I like it."

"That's good because you're stuck with it."

I raise my eyebrows at the statement.

"You're not stuck with us but let's just say guys will give you more space with our marks on you."

"Oh, so you're claiming me even if I don't claim you?" I ask, when he climbs on top of me, working teasing kisses from my stomach up between my breasts and over my neck.

"Pretty much. We've been around a long time. We know when something special lands at our feet and we're not letting you go easily."

"Show me. Show me who I belong to." I rasp when he bites my bottom lip, drawing blood.

"Little Creature, you're playing with fire." He growls, eyes flashing when he pulls back from the demanding kiss.

" Then let me burn."

A grin spreads across his face that makes me rethink my choice for a split second.

"I've been waiting my whole life to hear those words."

He takes my mouth roughly, deeply. His tongue explores every untouched spot, flooding my mouth with venom and turning me into a quivering mess.

"You heard her Nick." He growls when he pulls back. He's quick to circle his arms around my body and flip us just as the venom hits my nervous system.

"You want both of us, don't you?" Nick teases his finger around my back entrance, causing me to squeak.

"You can handle both of us. You want his knot inside you." Lucifer sucks my lip into his mouth, lapping at the sore spot he made earlier.

"Yes."

"Yes, what?"

"I want both of you."

"That's not what I want to hear, Pet." Lucifer growls.

"Please fuck me together. I want both of your cocks, please." I beg as Lucifer lifts my hips and sinks his searing hot cock deep in my cunt on the first stroke.

"Listen to the little whore beg. She wants you to knot her ass, Nick."

"I heard and I'm about to cum just thinking about how tight she's going to squeeze me."

Lucifer's fingers reach around to spread my cheeks, making me lean forward and present my ass to the big man behind me.

"Make sure she's good and ready first."

The first lick of that lovely tongue starts at my clit before working up to where my body is joined with the Devil's.

"If you keep that up, I'm going to fill her up before you even get the tip in." Lucifer grunts.

"I can feel his tongue wrapped around you and sliding inside me." I groan, leaning more into his hard chest.

"Yes. He's teasing both of us."

"Just had to remind you who's in charge. " Nick laughs.

"Please, stop teasing. I need you." I moan when his tongue slides over the sensitive spot inside me.

"Only because you ask so nicely."

He swipes his tongue over my ass, wetting me thoroughly before sinking a thick fingers inside me.

"I have to stretch you if you want to take my knot." He informs me when he slips another finger beside the first and works them in unison.

Pumping me, swirling them inside me, stretching me open all while Lucifer fucks me slowly.

"Please! I want you." I beg.

"Be still." He grabs my hips with one hand and lines the tip of his cock up with the other.

"Deep breath and remember to push back on me." He groans when he begins to slide in.

The fullness is immaculate. His cock matches perfectly with Lucifer's and it's the most complete I've felt in a long time.

"I'm about halfway."

My eyes pop open at this information.

"You can't be. It won't go anymore."

"I'm not stopping until you're stretched over my knot."

"Kiss me." Lucifer hisses and I quickly dive into his mouth, licking up every drop of venom.

With the next push it feels like I might actually rip in half.

"Almost." Nick's grunts.

"Stop!"

And he does. He freezes in that very spot, my ass still feeling like a hot poker is rimming me.

"Just take a minute and breathe. We're almost there." Lucifer coaches. Kissing my face and throat as I break out in a cold sweat.

"I'm going to keep moving Red. It'll be better once I'm in and you can relax." He assures me.

I grit my teeth and push back on the giant cock when I finally feel the pop of his knot fitting inside me.

"You are so deep. I can feel you everywhere." I pant.

"You wanted to burn." Lucifer smirks before he begins the deep thrusting that makes me fall over on top of him.

My body is jelly.

My brain is overloaded with the venom, the pain and the delicious feel of Nick's knot rubbing against Lucifer's cock.

I lay there and get used like the dirty little slut I want

to be.

I could see days spent like this.

They use me for their pleasure while I steal my own.

"Fuck you are so tight. You're going to drain me." Nick snarls, grabbing my hair and pulling me up to lick at the mark he left in my neck.

"Fill her up. I want to feel your cock pulse." Lucifer groans, hips jerking in time with Nick's.

"You want me to fill your tight little ass up?"

"Yes. Please! I can't handle it anymore." I beg.

"Well, you're going to be shit out of luck. We'll be locked together for a while after this."

I squirm back at the idea, silently begging for him to do it.

"Fine by me." He grunts, pulling my hair until my scalp burns and fucking me harder than I've ever been fucked.

"Fuck. He feels so good swelled inside you." Lucifer's eyes roll back as his claws sink into my hips. His cock swells as he cums deep in my cunt.

His orgasm makes everything tighter and the knot drags over something inside me that makes my vision go black.

"Fuck, so close." I cry.

"That's it. Squeeze my knot. Such a good girl." Nick groans as his knot swells even bigger. His words combined with the fullness deep inside me makes the world the light up behind my eyelids.

I cum so hard my whole body convulses on their cocks but I'm locked on. No where I can go to escape the extreme pressure.

"That's it. Drain me." Nick moans as his cock pulses one last time.

"You look like a goddess." Lucifer smiles up at me but my body has completely given up, as I fall down on him and try my best to relax while the knot the size of my fist sits in my ass.

"I feel like a sweaty mess." I groan into his shoulder.

"Yes, but still goddess-like in all your sweaty glory."

"Thanks. So, what now?" I ask when they slowly turn us to our sides. Every pull of the knot makes my stomach tingle.

"We'll lay here until you're free. So, try to relax or we'll be here all night." Nick smiles, his lips find my ear and nibbles.

"Then stop doing that." I laugh and squirm.

"Never." He growls playfully.

"Post DP looks so good on you." Lucifer kisses my throat.

"It is very nice. I had got used to rushing to the bathroom as soon as it was over. Michael pitched a fit if I got his sheets messy."

"I'm starting to think Michael needs a lesson in how to treat a lady." Nick says, stretching and shifting his knot inside me.

"Says the guy that just got done using my body and calling me a slut." I laugh.

"But you enjoyed it. That's the difference."

"True but I don't want either of you fighting with him. He's not worth it."

"No fighting. Pinky promise." Lucifer smirks and I can see the glimmer of mischief in his eyes.

"Uh huh. You're the devil. I know better than to trust the devil."

"Some witches worship the devil but leave it to me to get the one that likes to smart off." He rolls his eyes.

"Oh hush. You already said you like me being a brat." I smile at him as Nick chuckles behind me.

"She's got you there."

"Well, I like to spank your bratty little ass." He groans as he sways my hip making me yelp.

"Either way, no fighting with Angel boy." I reiterate.

"I said no fighting. I mean it."

"Then what do you mean?" I quirk an eyebrow.

"He means we are going into fuck with him. Completely harmless of course." Nick smiles against the back of my neck, making me forget the argument on my tongue.

"We'll get back to this conversation later. We have other things to deal with." Lucifer grinds his hardening cock against my stomach.

"We still have ten days of Yuletide fun." I remind them.

"And many more days after that." Nick groans as I clench around his knot.

"No matter what, this has been one hell of a yule."

Who Wants Another Slice Of Pie?

"**Y**ou sure he's not home?" I whisper to Nick as we slink through the pitch-black house.

"I'm positive. He's out with that choir angel. Probably having a really boring dinner." He whispers back.

"Then why are we whispering?"

"Just in case."

"Well, what about..."

His groan cuts me short.

"Will you please just be quiet and stay behind me."

"Okay, okay." I put my hands up in surrender, following his every footstep through the house.

"It's in that room." I whisper over his shoulder, pointing to the big white door to the right of him.

"Okay. Let's make it quick. He probably has alarms set." He answers, turning the knob and swinging the door open.

"What the fuck?"

He freezes and I'm forced to peek over his shoulder.

In the middle of the big trophy room Lucifer stands, a huge metal suit strapped to his body and Michaels flaming sword clutched in his fists.

"I found it! Look at this neat suit that was with it!"

"What are you doing?" Nick shakes his head but I see the corner of his mouth lifting as he turns to quietly shut the door.

"I'm Michael but back when he was sort of a badass. Waaa!" He screams as he swings the sword at an invisible enemy.

"Ooohhh. Does he have another?" I ask, scooting by Nick to inspect the armor and sword.

"I haven't looked. I've been busy fighting back Hell's legion." He swings the sword again, flames fanning around him.

"What's this?" I see a glass case under the shelves filled with artifacts.

I pull out a long staff with a sharp blade attached to the end.

"That's my spear! That son of a bitch said he didn't have it." He growls as I take up a fighting stance and pretend to stab at him with the spear.

"On guard!"

"You are insane. We have to get out of here." Nick groans, rubbing his palms over his eyes in frustration.

"We're badass fighting angels! Come on Saint Nick. Have some fun!" Lucifer smiles, passing the sword to Nick who looks it over before grabbing it.

"Only for a minute." He murmurs to himself, swinging the sword like a kid with a new toy.

"This is fucking awesome!" He laughs as he makes fighting noises.

BAM!

The door falls off its hinges when a giant red demon kicks it down.

"No one moves and maybe I won't shoot your ass." A petite purple woman screams as she makes her way around the big one.

"Cherry, put your gun away. These are not the people." A beautiful gray skinned man appears out of thin air beside the fuming woman.

"You don't know that for sure." She grumbles but puts her gun in its holster anyway.

"My visions are messed up but I know that these people didn't do it."

"Do what? Who are you?" Nick asks, getting angry.

"That sword you're holding was used in a homicide and we are the people that take care of things like that." The big red one answers.

"We are agents for P.I.E. Paranormal Investigation and Enforcement and we're here for Michael."

The End

Want to know more about P.I.E?
Read all about Cherry and her men here.
P.I.E